ANNA LIZA

and the

HAPPY

PRACTICE

ANNA LIZA

and the HAPPY PRACTICE

Eoin Colfer

Illustrated by
Matt Robertson

Barrington  Stoke

First published in 2021 in Great Britain by
Barrington Stoke Ltd
18 Walker Street, Edinburgh, EH3 7LP

www.barringtonstoke.co.uk

This 4u2read edition based on *Anna Liza and the Happy
Practice* (Barrington Stoke, 2016)

Text © 2016 & 2021 Artemis Fowl Ltd
Illustrations © 2016 Matt Robertson

A CIP catalogue record for this book is available
from the British Library upon request

ISBN: 978-1-80090-052-3

Printed by Hussar Books, Poland

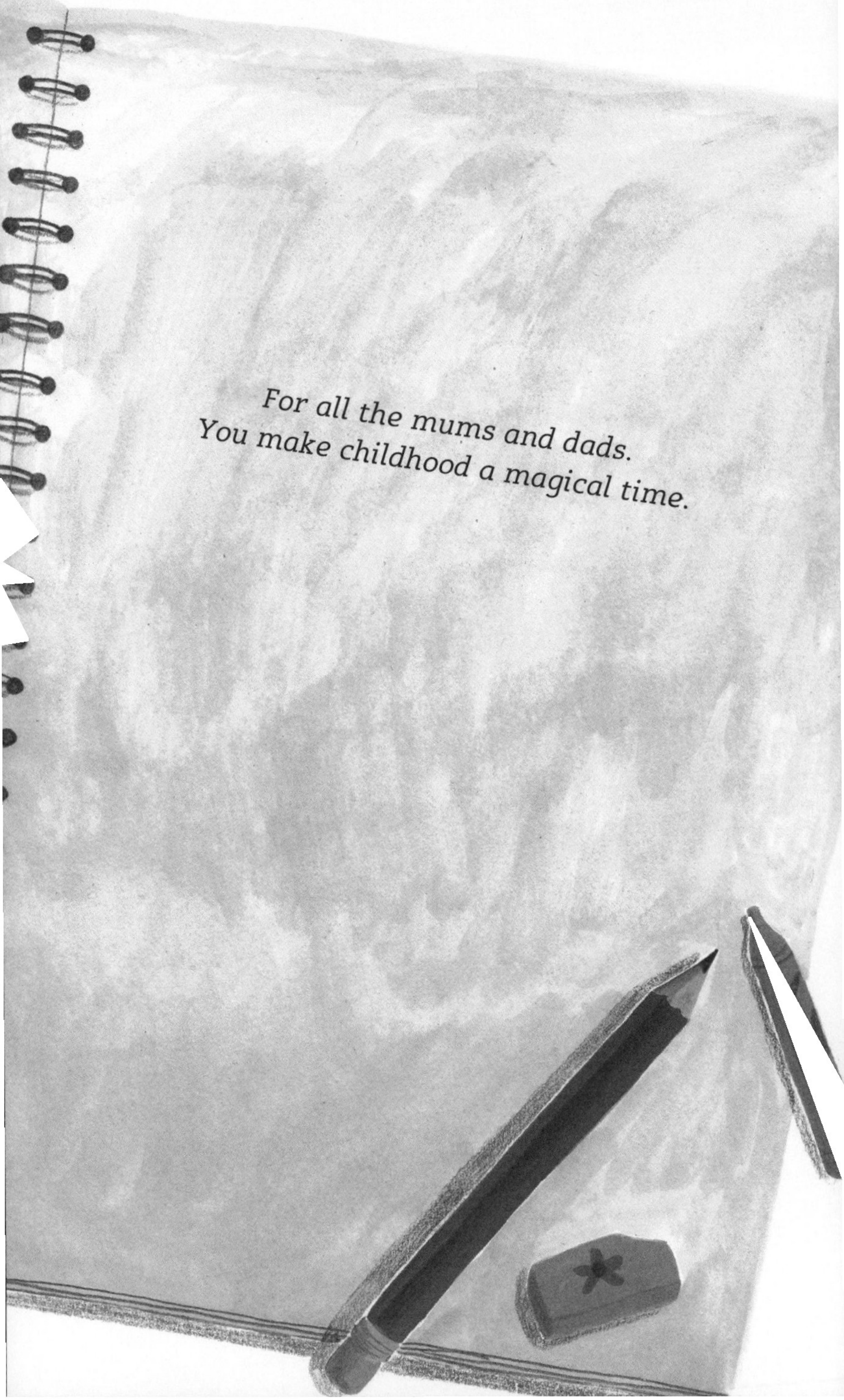

For all the mums and dads.
You make childhood a magical time.

Contents

CHAPTER 1

Practise, Practise, Practise

There are all sorts of doctors.

Doctors for cuts.

Doctors for bruises.

There are even doctors who can check out the inside of your body with tiny cameras.

My mum is none of those.

My mum is a brain doctor. She doesn't poke around in people's brains. But what my mum does is talk with people who are really upset or very lonely, until they feel better.

Mum says that it's more important to listen to her patients than to talk to them.

Doctors like my mum are called ... wait ... it's a really long word.

Are you ready for this?

It took me a whole week to learn how to spell it.

Doctors like my mum are called psychiatrists. (You don't say the P. You say sye-kye-a-trist.)

I think that a job where you can make sad people happy again must be the best job in the world and I want to be a psychiatrist too.

I asked Mum if I could be one right now, but she told me that only big people who have practised for years and years can be psychiatrists. So that means that I have to practise for years if I want to make people happy.

And I'm going to start doing that right away.

So that's me. I am Anna Liza Madigan, practising psychiatrist – and my office is in my mother's waiting room. I call it the Happy Practice.

CHAPTER 2

Don't Worry, Be Happy

Every day after school I do my rounds in
Mum's waiting room. I like to look like a
proper doctor, so I wear the stethoscope and
white coat from my "Nurse Nancy on Duty" set.

Most days I get people cups of water and
maybe a magazine to read while they wait.
But sometimes if a person seems really sad,
I sit next to them and sing them a song like

"Don't Worry, Be Happy". That makes most people smile.

But one day a little boy sat in the waiting room while his dad was in my mum's office. I got him a glass of water and some grapes and I sang him my Top 3 songs, but I couldn't change the sad look on his face into a happy one. So I sat down beside him.

"I am Anna Liza," I said, and I held out my hand. "I'll be your doctor today."

The boy shook my hand.

"I'm Edward," he said. "I am seven point five years old and I don't like ketchup on my burgers."

I wrote this down in my notebook along with Edward's address, which was only two streets away at the top of the hill. Mum says that you never know what fact might be the key to helping someone.

Edward was the saddest person I had ever seen. His eyes were red from crying and he could not smile a tiny smile even when I told him my Top 17 knock-knock jokes.

In fact, Edward didn't even say the "Who's there?" bit when I said "Knock, knock," and I had to do the whole joke myself.

It looked like I needed to know more.

"What seems to be the problem, Edward?" I asked him.

For a long time Edward didn't say a word and I thought he might be having a nap until he whispered, "It's my dad."

A dad problem. Dad and mum problems happen a lot. Half the children I talk to in the waiting room have a dad or mum problem.

"Hmm," I said, and I wrote "Dad Problem" in my Nurse Nancy notebook.

"I'm sad because Daddy's sad," Edward said. And I guessed by the wobble in his lip that he was going to burst out crying any second.

This was bad for two reasons:

1. I hate to see people cry as it often makes me cry.

And:

2. Mum says that if I make any more
patients cry with my terrible jokes,
she will strip me of my Nurse Nancy
stethoscope.

Number 2 is very unfair as my jokes are really
good. For example:

Knock knock.

Who's there?

Avenue.

Avenue who?

Avenue got a smile for me?

That is hilarious. And useful. Mum should pay
me for my jokes.

"Don't cry, Edward," I said, and I passed him a tissue from a box on the coffee table.

"Do you know why your dad is so sad?" I asked.

Edward blew his nose and handed back the tissue.

"I think it's because my mum is gone, Doctor," he said. "Dad gets sad and then I get sad."

Doctor! Edward called me "Doctor". That's the first time I've been called Doctor. I tried to stay calm.

"What happens when your daddy gets sad?" I asked.

Edward sniffed. "He just sits on the couch and says stuff like, 'My life isn't going anywhere.'"

I wrote this down too: "Edward's dad says his life is not going anywhere."

Interesting.

Edward had another interesting fact for me.

"Sometimes," he said, "I get up early just so I can have a few hours alone without anyone being sad."

This was so sad that I bet the two of us would have started to cry right then and there if Mum's office door hadn't clicked open. I hid behind a chair before she could see me treating Edward, or, as she calls it, "Bothering the people in the waiting room."

Edward saw me hiding. "Can't you help me, Doctor?" he said.

I whispered. "Of course. I'll come and see you when my plan is ready."

And when he heard this, Edward smiled, just a little bit.

CHAPTER 3

A Dad Problem

You bet I was going to help Edward with his dad problem.

Anyone who calls me "Doctor" twice in one appointment deserves all the help I have to give. So I cancelled the rest of my appointments (which were with my dolls and goldfish anyway), and I thought about Edward's daddy.

I read my notes on "Patient 1 – Edward".
They said:

Edward does not like ketchup on his burgers.

Perhaps something bad had happened to him with ketchup when he was a baby.

I moved on:

Edward has a dad problem.

So did I. But his was much worse. My dad problem was that Daddy would not take me sky-diving because I was only nine years old.

Edward's dad says his life is not going anywhere.

Not going anywhere.

What could I do about a person who wasn't going anywhere?

What did I do when I needed to go somewhere?

Hmmm.

A plan popped into my head. A plan so clever that I could sell it to Mum to use on her patients. But I had tried to sell Mum my plans before and she had said things like:

"Absolutely not, Anna Liza."

"It's far too dangerous."

Or her favourite:

"Before we start discussing your treatment ideas, why don't we discuss your homework?"

So maybe I would tell Mum about the plan after it had worked. Brilliantly. Because I knew it would work brilliantly.

I knew just the way to treat Edward's daddy. I knew exactly how to make his life go somewhere.

CHAPTER 4

Good Morning, Doctor

The next day was Saturday, so I dressed in my Nurse Nancy white coat, packed my bag and crept out of the house.

The sun was just coming up over the hilltop where Edward lived and I hoped this would be one of those mornings where he got up early for some happy time.

It took longer than I thought it would to get to Edward's house because the hill was steep and I took three breaks to look down the hill to the sea. Daddy always says the sea is blue and sparkly like my eyes. It is very nice to have a happy daddy.

Edward's house was a big blue one, with windows that looked like eyes and a front door that looked like a mouth.

I sneaked around the side and peeped in the kitchen window. There was Edward eating Coco Pops from the box and reading a book with a big boom explosion on the cover.

I tapped on the window and Edward did not get a fright like I would if someone tapped on my window.

He just put down the book and pointed to the back door. I walked around the back to meet him.

"Good morning, Doctor," he said, and we shook hands.

"How is your daddy?" I asked him.

Edward rubbed his sleepy eyes. "Daddy's asleep."

"Good," I said. "Take me to him, but we must move without a sound. Like ninjas."

Edward must have been a ninja fan because as he climbed the stairs he spun from side to side and kicked out at invisible enemies.

I didn't tell him he didn't need to do that because it looked like he was enjoying himself.

Edward's daddy was lying on his bed with his feet sticking out the end, which was perfect for what I had in mind. I put my bag on the floor and took out my big brother's roller-skates.

"Now," I whispered. "We need to put these roller-skates on your daddy's feet, but we mustn't wake him up."

Edward frowned and I could see he wasn't sure if that was a good idea.

"Trust me, Edward," I said. "I'm your doctor."

And Edward whispered, "OK."

He took one of the roller-skates and slipped it onto his daddy's left foot while I did the right foot. It's lucky most kids are very good at

being sneaky. We did up both roller-skates and Edward's dad did not wake up.

When we were finished, Edward made a face at me. It was one of those faces with a question inside, and the question was: "What now?"

"Now you open the front door," I told him.

Edward went downstairs, still doing all his ninja moves.

When I heard the front door open, I started on the last bit of my plan. I took my bicycle horn out of my bag – one of those ones with a rubber bulb that you squeeze to make the horn toot.

I held the horn close to Edward's daddy's ear, then squeezed the bulb hard.

"TOOT! TOOT!" said the horn.

"Aaaaaaargh!" said Edward's daddy, and he shot out of bed.

I tried to remember exactly how he said it so I could write it down in my notebook.

In my plan, Edward's daddy skated to the stairs by himself, but in real life he needed a push.

"You can thank me later," I called after him as he bounced down the stairs, out the front door and straight down the hill.

"You see," I called to Edward, proud of myself. "Now your daddy's life is going somewhere."

CHAPTER 5

Omelette

We ran outside and watched Edward's daddy zoom down the hill towards the sea.

This is brilliant, I thought to myself.

"Will Daddy be OK?" Edward asked. "He's not a very good skater."

"He'll be fine," I told him. "My mum always says that you can't make an omelette without breaking a few legs."

Edward frowned. "I don't understand that."

"Me neither," I admitted. "But I do like omelettes."

We climbed onto the garden wall and tried to watch Edward's dad as he zig-zagged away down the town.

He crashed into a garden hedge and came out the other side with leaves in his hair.

Then he smacked into the bakery boy who was carrying the morning bread on a big tray.

"That's great," I said to Edward. "Bread is full of carbs, and carbs give you energy."

Down the hill went Edward's dad, swinging his arms to keep himself from tipping over and calling to the people as he passed.

Edward's dad was having so much fun that I was a bit jealous.

He skated up a builder's plank and flew into the air. He landed on the back of a sand lorry which was tipping sand into a big hole in the road.

Edward's dad was tipped out with the sand and only just missed being dumped into the hole. Instead he zoomed off down the hill, his pyjamas flapping in the wind.

Then he met the tram that takes people down our hill to the harbour. He hung on to the rail while tourists took photos of him.

When the tram turned left, Edward's dad went straight on into the middle of a flock of seagulls that flapped all around his body like a bird-jacket.

If only the birds would carry Edward's dad into the sky, I thought. Instead they flew off with his pyjama top and left him to rattle and bump along the planks of the pier.

Edward's mouth was hanging open. He looked like he was properly impressed with my plan. At last he moved his mouth. "I can't believe this," he said.

"I know," I said. I was so proud. "I thought he would crash long before now."

Edward's dad flew off the end of the pier like a ski-jumper and went up and up for the longest time before he splashed down into the deep blue sea. He made a fizz of white bubbles where he landed.

"I think I heard a scream," Edward said.

"You have good hearing," I said. I would have to add this fact to my notes.

CHAPTER 6

Burgers at Patty Cake

It took Edward's dad longer to get back up the hill than it had taken him to go down, but not much longer. This was because, after some fishermen helped him out of the water, he ran all the way back to the house.

"Did you see me?" he called to Edward. "Did you see me, son?"

Edward jumped down from the wall. "I saw you, Daddy. You were cool."

I could see a lot of Edward's dad's teeth, but I didn't know if he was happy or angry.

"Yes," Edward's dad said. "I was cool, wasn't I? But I didn't know what was happening. I still don't."

"I liked the part with the birds," said Edward.

Edward's dad pointed to his elbow, which had a little cut on it. "One of them pecked me," he said, and he had a proper smile on his face now. "I couldn't believe it. I haven't done anything like that, well, ever. But we did things before, son, didn't we?"

"We sure did," Edward said. "I liked doing things."

"So did I," said his dad. "I had forgotten what it's like with the wind in your hair and the sea. Oh my goodness, the sea. I love swimming and you love it. Why haven't we been swimming for so long?"

I thought that I should answer that, as Edward's practising psychiatrist. "You've been sad, Edward's dad," I said. "Ever since Edward's mum left."

Edward's dad looked over at me then, perhaps because I had just said something. He knew me, of course, from Mum's waiting room.

"You're right," he said. "I have been sad. And I am sad, but I have Edward and I love him." He gave Edward a big hug and, even

though his dad was soaking wet, Edward
smiled.

"I have you, son," Edward's dad said. "And
I love you, and as I crashed into the bread boy
and landed on the sand lorry, all I could think

was *Edward, Edward, Edward*, over and over again. All I could think about was you and how much I missed us doing stuff."

This was really good news, but for some reason Edward started to cry. I thought I'd better try to say something to help.

"So, Edward's dad, would you say your life is going places now?" I asked.

Edward's dad did not need to think about this for very long.

"Yes," he said. "My life is going places and so is Edward's." He stopped hugging Edward. "Get your swimming trunks and bucket," he said. "We're going to the beach."

"The beach," Edward said, because he couldn't believe it.

"Yes, the beach, and after for burgers at Patty Cake."

This was a good idea. At Patty Cake's they give you burgers with no ketchup.

"Well," I said. "I think my work here is done."

Edward's dad frowned at me. "I don't really know what you've been up to, Anna Liza."

I made a serious face. "The mind is a puzzling place," I said. "Have fun at the beach."

Edward's dad went inside to dry off and Edward shook my hand.

"Thanks, Doctor," he said. "You did a great job."

"You're welcome, Edward," I said. "I am your practising psychiatrist after all."

"How much do I owe you?" he asked.

"I'll send you a bill," I said. "I accept chocolate, crayons, second-hand books or fancy paper. I collect fancy paper."

Edward nodded. "I better go," he said as he went inside. "I don't want to miss one minute of Dad being happy."

"I think that's a good idea," I said.

Edward ran into the house and I walked back down the hill with a big happy smile on my face. About halfway down the hill I stopped smiling because I remembered my brother's roller-skates. They were still in the sea.

CHAPTER 7

Promise

I tried to sell Mum the roller-skate treatment, but she didn't agree with me that it was a genius idea.

"You are never to do anything like that again, Anna Liza," she said. "We're lucky that Edward's dad isn't going to take us to court. When he and Edward get back from their holiday in Hawaii, you will march straight up there and say sorry. Understood?"

I nodded. While I was there, I could do a follow-up with Edward.

"No more roller-skate treatments!" Mum said. "Promise."

"I promise, no more roller-skate treatments."

"I know you were trying to help," Mum said. "But psychiatry can be tricky. It's for proper doctors only."

I nodded again. Mum likes it when I nod and don't argue.

"If you want to help, you can ask the next patient to come in," she said. "Would you like that?"

"Yes, Mum," I said, and I opened my eyes as wide as I could, which I happen to know makes me look extra cute.

Mum laughed. "Don't think those big eyes will work on me, Anna Liza."

But they did work and Mum gave me a big kiss on the cheek.

"OK, my little junior psychiatrist," she said. "Send in the next person."

I went into the waiting room and there sat a woman in a green coat with a little girl who had to be her daughter.

"The doctor will see you now," I said.

The woman nodded and stood up slowly, as if standing was difficult for her. She went into the office without a word to her daughter.

I sat beside her daughter. The chair was still warm from the last bottom.

"Hi," I said. "Knock knock?"

The girl didn't answer. She just looked down at her shoes. Why didn't she look at mine instead? They were pink with dolphins on them.

"Don't you like knock-knock jokes?" I asked her.

The girl shook her head. "I don't like any jokes since my mum got sad."

I knew that I should walk away, but I couldn't help myself. After all, I am the Happy Practice's only doctor.

"I see, and what happens when your mum is sad?" I asked.

The girl shook her head. "Nothing really. She just lies in bed and says that she feels stuck in one place."

Stuck in one place. Interesting.

Mum made me promise not to use the roller-skate treatment any more. But she didn't say anything about skateboards.

I took out my notebook.

"My name is Anna Liza Madigan," I said.
"And I'll be your practising psychiatrist today."

Our books are tested
for children and young people by
children and young people.

Thanks to everyone who consulted on
a manuscript for their time and effort in
helping us to make our books better
for our readers.

Anna Liza loves helping people who are struggling with their feelings. If you're struggling with how you feel and need to talk, you can call these free helplines for children and young people. They offer comfort, advice and protection.

Childline (UK)
0800 1111

Childline Ireland (Republic of Ireland)
1800 66 66 66